PROTECTING HIS SECRET BABY
SUNSET SECURITY BOOK THREE

SADIE KING

PROTECTING HIS SECRET BABY

SUNSET SECURITY

He's an ex-military security guard with a drinking problem. She's hiding a secret that may be his salvation.

I came back from the Army a broken man, carrying so much darkness that only the memory of one perfect weekend with Jodie kept me going.

But I've been back for nine months, and I've searched every bar on the Sunset Coast. She can't be found—or she doesn't want to be.

Until the day she turns up at my work as beautiful as I remember but remote. She doesn't want anything to do with me.

But the more she pushes me away, the greater my need grows.

I don't care what she's hiding. I'm never giving up on Jodie.

Protecting His Secret Baby is a steamy secret-baby, age-gap romance featuring an ex-military hero and the curvy woman who heals his heart.

DON'T MISS OUT!

Want to be the first to hear about new releases and special offers?

Follow Sadie King on BookBub to get an alert whenever she has a new release, preorder, or discount!

www.bookbub.com/authors/sadie-king

1
KIEREN

The music lulls before the next song from the jukebox kicks in, and over the noise of slurred voices and glasses clinking, I hear the click-clack of high heels behind me.

My heartbeat picks up a notch, and I set my drink down on the bar with trembling hands. My brain tells me that it's not her. Jodie wore flat sandals. They were fiery orange with crsiss-cross straps that matched her summer dress. But my body hasn't caught up.

I turn around slowly, just in case. Because maybe the flat sandals and simple style weren't her usual attire. In the eighteen months since I met Jodie, maybe—just maybe—she's taken to wearing killer heels and frequenting bars until closing time.

The owner of the heels wears a tight-fitting sparkly dress that ends well above the thigh. It shimmers as she walks toward me on diamante-encrusted high heels. The overall impression is of a disco ball, which makes me smile to myself.

Big mistake.

The woman thinks I'm smiling at her, and in my beer-hazy head, I don't look away fast enough.

She gives me a slow smile and lowers her mascara-coated lashes. Her makeup is smeared in dark smudges around her eyes, and her lipstick is half worn off.

"Hey there," she says.

At that moment, the music kicks in, and she leans forward as if we're in the middle of an intimate discussion and not strangers at a bar.

"What's that?"

Her breath smells of strong alcohol and the garlic mayo they serve with chicken wings at the bar.

"I didn't say anything," I mumble.

"My name's Lisa," she continues despite me turning back to the bar and taking a long gulp of beer.

When I don't offer my name, Lisa sidles onto the stool next to mine as if my silence is an invitation, as if she likes a challenge and I'm her chosen target for tonight.

"I saw you earlier, sitting here alone all night."

I pull at the label on my beer bottle, wondering how to get rid of Lisa without hurting her feelings.

"I'm looking for someone."

I realize too late that's the wrong thing to say because Lisa shuffles forward on her stool and leans on the bar with her left elbow so that her boobs are practically in my face. I pointedly ignore them.

"You just found her."

Lisa is definitely not the woman I'm looking for. Jodie was sweet and natural with a lopsided smile and dancing eyes.

Lisa rests her hand on my arm and gives it a small squeeze while giving me what I guess is supposed to be a coy smile but, from a woman who's clearly had too much to drink, comes out like a maniacal grin.

PROTECTING HIS SECRET BABY

How easy it would be to go home with Lisa. To lose myself in a stranger for an hour or two. To forget Jodie and her haunting smile and the way her lips brushed mine and how good it felt to lie with her body next to mine.

The thought of Jodie makes my heart hurt and turns any encounter with another woman into a non-starter. How could I be with anyone else when I know Jodie is out there somewhere?

"I'm sorry." I take Lisa's hand off mine and place it on the bar. "I'm not interested."

Jodie's eyes flash dangerously, and her mouth closes in a thin line.

"You'd be lucky to get a chance with someone like me."

I've offended her, and she's not going to take it easily. I should get up and leave, walk out of the bar and go home. But I've had way too many beers to do anything so sensible, and I feel a little annoyed.

Who does this woman think she is? Just because a guy's drinking alone, she thinks he's looking for a hookup? Just because she offers herself to a man, she thinks he should take her up on it?

"Doesn't seem like it's that hard to get a chance with you."

I should stop. I shouldn't offend the poor woman, but I'm drunk and I'm hurting and I can't stop myself.

"Excuse me?"

She puts her hands on her hips and her voice is raised, drawing the attention of the whole bar. "Are you calling me easy?"

Walk away, Kieren. Walk away, walk away, walk away.

This time, I listen to my drink-addled brain and put my hands up while I slide off my barstool. I don't notice the man who's come up behind me until I back into him.

I'm a decent-sized man, but this guy is huge. At least a foot taller than me and twice as wide with muscles in his arms that pop out of the tight t-shirt he's wearing. His bushy eyebrows are drawn together in an angry line.

"What did you call my sister?"

Oh, great. She's got Popeye for a brother and he's pissed off.

Lisa's wearing a smirk, which tells me she's enjoying the trouble she's caused. Maybe these two work as a team praying on drunk men. I don't know what their angle is, but I do know I never back down from a fight.

"I didn't mean to offend your sister."

That's when Popeye makes a fatal mistake.

I may only be five foot eight, but I'm wiry. My body is honed from years in the Special Forces, and I know how to fight.

Popeye pushes me in the chest in the way that only large men do to smaller men they're trying to intimidate.

Big mistake.

In one move, I spin around with an upper cut to the chest and a kick that's supposed to connect with his side belly. Only I'm too drunk and slow. Popeye takes the punch with a heave and doubles over but manages to dodge the kick.

He throws a punch that I'm too slow to dodge, and it clips me on the side of the ear. The force spins me around, and I'm too drunk to keep my balance.

I stagger backwards, falling onto a table and sending glasses crashing to the floor.

I try to stand up, but the room is spinning, and instead I slump to the floor.

Popeye is bearing down on me, but Dave, the barman, steps in front of him with his arms crossed and a furious look on his face.

The room is hazy, and I'm not sure if I'm sitting on the floor or leaning against the bar.

"Let's go, Kieren."

The voice is familiar, and I squint into the face of Seth, my best friend. Even with his bad leg, Seth manages to pull me up because I'm fuck-all useless in this state.

My head is fuzzy, and I'm not sure what just happened.

I'm vaguely aware of Seth throwing some cash on the bar. "To cover the damage." Which makes me wonder. What damage?

Then he's shoving me through the door, and the cool, fresh air hits my face, making me want to puke.

I run to a bin and retch into it, but nothing comes out.

Laughing, I clutch the side of the bin and look up to find Seth with his arms folded, looking down at me like he's my angry dad.

"What the fuck was all that about?"

I shrug because I really don't know.

I went into the Sea Hopper looking for Jodie like I've been doing most nights since I got back from tour. But like every single night, she wasn't there.

She hasn't been at any other bar or cafe or restaurant. I've tried them all in a fifty-mile radius up and down the coast. But I keep coming back to the Sea Hopper, the place where we met eighteen months ago, the place where our one incredible weekend started and ended.

But Seth's looking at me like I'm a naughty child, not his colleague in the security firm and brother in arms from our Special Forces days. A thought occurs to me.

"How did you know I was there?"

Seth looks away, and I know he's been up to no good. He's the IT expert in our security firm. I know he doesn't always use ethical means.

"I was watching on the CCTV."

That doesn't surprise me, but I am touched by his dedication to keeping me out of trouble.

"You were checking up on me?"

SADIE KING

"Someone has to."

He takes my arm and leads me to his car.

"You've got to pull yourself together, Kieren. You can't keep pulling shit like this. If Bronn found out, you could be off the team."

That's a sobering thought. Bronn runs the security firm he set up for his old Special Forces team once we all got out of the military.

Security is a good job for a man who's only ever known the military. But since my one weekend with Jodie, I find it hard to care about anything else. If I just knew where she was, I could stop this stupid search, going to bars every night and drinking more than I should.

"Why don't you just let me look her up for you?"

It's as if Seth can read my mind, which wouldn't be too hard since it's been stuck on the Jodie page for the last eighteen months.

It's not the first time Seth has offered to find her for me. Sure, I've looked her up on social media, but it's hard to find a woman when you only know her first name. There are a lot of Jodies in the state, and none of them are her.

We kept it impersonal on purpose, believing it was a one-off thing. But Jodie ran off before I told her I wanted more. Then I was deployed, and now she's vanished without a trace.

"I don't want you invading her privacy."

Because hacking into God knows what to find her is something I can't get behind. It may have worked for Seth to get his woman, but I won't disrespect Jodie's privacy that way.

"Suit yourself, man." We reach Seth's car and I slide into the passenger seat. "But you've got to stop getting into trouble like this. If you want me to help you find her, I will find her. But if you don't want me to, then you've got to let her go. You've got to move on."

He starts up the engine, and we ride in silence to my place. I stare out the window at the lights going past and know there is no way in hell that I'll ever move on from Jodie.

2
JODIE

"Will three changes be enough, or should I pack four?"

The phone's on speaker on the bed, and even though I can't see her, I can feel Clare's eyeroll.

"Stop stressing already."

Holding up a stained bodysuit, I discard it and rifle through the drawer, looking for something that is clean and not too worn. I can't send Layla to daycare on her first day in dirty clothes.

"I just want it to go smoothly for her."

"Three changes will be enough. What's the worst that can happen? They put her in a spare set from the lost and found and you have lots of washing to do?"

My sister's comments are supposed to be comforting, but all it does is remind me of the water bill that's overdue and the fact I'm having to ration the heating to one hot bath a week because it's all I can afford.

"You're right. Three should be enough."

But I stuff an extra pair of diapers into the already bursting bag. Just in case.

PROTECTING HIS SECRET BABY

"I wish I could be there for my niece's first day of daycare. Are you going to be okay?"

I know Clare means well, but she's halfway down the country on her first tour and I don't want to saddle her with my worries.

It's been just the two of us for as long as I can remember, and I had to forcibly make her take the job or she wouldn't have left me and Layla on our own. Her theatre group is touring its show around the state, and I couldn't ask her to turn down the opportunity.

I wish you could be here too, I silently say. But I don't want Clare to know how bad things have gotten here.

"We'll be fine. I'm really looking forward to starting work."

I say it so brightly that I almost convince myself.

The truth us, I'm scared about leaving Layla with strangers. Sure, we've had settling in days at the daycare, but this is the first time in the nine months since she came into my life that I'll be away from her for more than an a few hours. And even then, it's only a five-hour shift.

There's a cry from the next room, letting me know that Layla doesn't like being left on her own.

"I better go, Clare. Good luck with the show tonight."

"Good luck with the daycare drop-off. Call if you need me."

We hang up, and I stuff my phone into my pocket and grab the overstuffed day bag.

Layla's in the next room where I left her propped up with cushions and her favorite caterpillar toy.

Her face lights up when she sees me, making my heart warm and letting me know that despite everything—despite wearing secondhand clothes and having hot water only on Sundays, despite giving up going out with friends, despite giving up everything but looking after her—it's all worth it.

"Hey, sweetie, you ready to go?"

I pick her up and shoulder the bag, which is way heavier than it should be. I have a fleeting worry that I haven't packed enough of her favorite snacks but rationalize that the daycare provides food so there's bound to be something she likes. I grab a banana and jam it in the front pocket of the bag just in case.

Then I'm out the door.

Bertha's the most beat-up car in the parking lot of our block of one and two-bedroom apartments. I strap Layla in and slide into the passenger seat, trying not to get my clothes caught on the wire springs that are poking through the vinyl seats in alarmingly increasing areas.

The engine makes a horrible chugging sound when I turn the key, and I pray to the car gods that whatever force has kept Bertha alive longer than she should continues to be strong and hold her together for just a few more months.

"Come on, Bertha."

A few more months is all I need. A few months of work to get the bills paid and put a little aside every month for a new car. Or at least a less old one.

The car gods must be listening because Bertha splutters to life.

"You beauty."

Layla giggles as I pat the dashboard affectionately, and I adjust my mirror to see her smile in the rearview. I could spend all day looking at that smile.

But I need to look after her in other ways, so unfortunately that's not an option anymore. Swallowing down my mother's guilt, I reverse out of the parking space.

It's a short drive to the daycare, the only one I could find with fees low enough to make going to work worthwhile.

I won't be earning much over what it costs me to send her there at first, but I'm confident that over time my income will increase and just getting back to working will be worth it.

We pull into the daycare parking lot, and as if sensing my concerns, Layla gives an uneasy wail.

"It's all right, sweetie. You're going to have a fun day today, meet new friends."

I hope she feels more reassured than I do. I get her out of the car and clasp her close as we walk up the steps.

The manager, Jan, comes out to greet us.

"Hello, Layla. You're going to spend the day with us."

Jan holds out her thick arms for Layla. This is where I'm supposed to let her go and let this kind woman take care of my baby. Instead, I find myself clutching Layla to my chest as a wave of possessiveness washes over me.

Jan sees my hesitation and smiles reassuringly.

"The first day is always the hardest," she says kindly but firmly.

Layla looks to Jan and gives her a wide smile, holding out her tubby fingers to her. Great. Even my own daughter is better at separation than I am.

Jan takes Layla around the waist but I still don't let go. I've never been without my baby for more than a few hours, and I'm struck by a sadness. It's like handing over a piece of my own heart.

"She'll be fine here. We'll look after her real well."

Jan is patient and kind, and she's right. Layla will be fine, and I need to do this. I need to let her go.

With great reluctance, I pry my hands off my baby. Jan pulls Layla toward her, and my treacherous daughter giggles, giving Jan one of her winning smiles.

"Aren't you a sweetheart," Jan coos.

"She sleeps at about ten and then again after lunch, but if you leave it too late, she gets fussy."

My voice breaks and I blink hard, willing myself not to cry.

"I know, Jodie," Jan says patiently. "We've got it all on the file."

Of course she does. I filled out forms and talked Jan through Layla's routine. These women are professionals. They know how to look after a baby.

"Wave bye-bye to Mommy."

Layla holds her fingers up to me, looking confused before Jan whisks her inside. Be quick, they told me. Don't prolong the goodbye and don't let her see you're upset.

I wait until the doors close behind them before I turn away, swiping at the corner of my eyes.

I know I have to get back to work and earn money to support my daughter, but dang, it feels like I just left a piece of my heart in there.

"Pull yourself together, girl," I mutter.

I've dealt with harder than this over the last eighteen months. I'll get through this too.

I sit in the car until the pain subsides and my eyes are dry. Now, it's time to get to work.

3
KIEREN

It feels like a freight train is rumbling through my head as I sip a strong cup of coffee in the briefing room the next morning.

We've just moved into new offices as the business expands, and Bronn's striding around like a proud peacock. I'm not sure how much of that is to do with the way his security firm is growing or the fact that he just found out his young wife is expecting their first child.

Either way, he's in an expansive mood and even giving out rare smiles, which is odd for my serious-minded boss.

Seth slides into the seat next to me and takes in my rumpled appearance and the large mug of black coffee I'm nursing.

"Morning," he says cheerfully, obviously taking great pleasure in my hangover.

"Morning—" I start to speak, but it comes out as a cough.

I hit myself on the chest to clear my throat. Bronn looks at me sharply.

"You coming down with something, Kieren?"

Seth stifles a laugh, and I shake my head, which sends the

SADIE KING

trains in my skull rumbling to the other side of my brain. It takes all my energy not to wince, but I can't show weakness in front of Bronn.

Thankfully, he's too caught up in the opening of the new office and our first briefing. He gives me a curt nod, and his gaze passes over me.

Relief floods me. Bronn is the typical hard-ass ex-soldier. He'd never understand what compels me to down liquor until I can't think straight, to escape into the sweet oblivion that alcohol brings.

I need to stop drinking. I know I need to. But try telling that to myself when I'm sitting in a bar and scouring every face, hoping that one of them is Jodie.

The thought I might have lost her forever grips me like a fear. My coffee tastes bitter in my mouth, and I suddenly want something stronger.

Jodie is what I thought about on my last and final deployment. She's what kept me sane. The memory of her soft voice, her smiling eyes, her body next to mine—it was the shining light that guided me through the darkness of war.

I always assumed I'd be able to find her when I got back. And if I don't, if there's no light, then there's only darkness.

Leo comes into the room, humming as he always does. The cheerful bastard. He clocks my hangover immediately and his eyes light up.

"Good night out, Kieren?" he teases. "Meet any women, or still flying solo?"

I flip him the bird, and he chuckles good naturedly. It's hard to be cross at Leo. When we were on tour, he kept us all going with his good humor and bad jokes.

Leo takes a seat at the back next to Tony, who's as sullen looking as Leo is cheerful. Tony grunts a greeting at Leo, keeping his giant arms folded, the bulges of his muscles making his tattoos fall at funny angles.

"Mmm, I suddenly have a strong urge to eat boiled eggs," Leo says jokingly, referring to Tony's completely bald head.

Tony started losing hair a few years ago and recently took the step to shave his head and be done with it. Leo never loses an opportunity to rib him about it.

If it was anyone else, Tony would have them in a headlock by now. But he and Leo grew up together. They're best friends and brothers in arms.

Tony just shakes his head heavily. "You gonna make that same joke every day, or you got any new material?"

"It's not a joke my friend. It's fact. I've got a boiled egg packed for lunch."

"Is that because you were thinking about me when you woke up?" Tony quips back. "That's sweet, man."

We all chuckle, enjoying the banter.

Bronn moves to the front of the room, and the chatter stops.

"Thank you all for coming in today," he starts.

There's some housekeeping about the new building, how parking works, fire safety, and all that. I try to concentrate but my mind wonders, as it always does, to Jodie.

I wonder what she's doing and where she is right now. If she's still on the coast or if she moved off somewhere. I'm regretting all the questions I never asked her on that one perfect weekend.

"Now that we've got a fancy new office," Bronn continues, "we've got a receptionist to field calls and greet clients."

The door opens, and a petite and curvy blonde comes through looking nervous.

"You've all met Amy before, the newest member of our team."

Leo sits up in his seat and nudges Tony. "You didn't tell me Amy was coming to work here?"

Tony looks hard at his daughter. "I can keep an eye on her here. Make sure no boys come sniffing around."

He cracks his knuckles, and I'd hate to be the man who tries to date his daughter.

"Hi, everyone." Amy gives a nervous smile.

I've known Amy since she was a baby. We all have. But you only see kids grow up in snapshots when you're in the military.

Especially if you're in the Special Forces. With long deployments and black comms, you can't always keep in touch with your family. Every time we came back, Amy would have grown up months at a time.

It's hard keeping a family together in those conditions, and it's not surprising Tony split with Amy's mom. It's not how he wanted things to go, but he loved her enough to set her free.

Now his little girl is all grown up, nineteen years old and our new receptionist.

"I'm sure you'll all make Amy feel welcome," Bronn says.

"Not too welcome," mutters Tony, and we all laugh.

Bronn gets to talking about the jobs this week and where we're all assigned.

I've got a cushy number ferrying around a visiting minor politician who's had death threats. Often, it's the presence of security that is the deterrent, but I won't be afraid to act to protect a client when I need to.

I'm zoning out again when the door to the briefing room opens.

Someone's pushing backwards into the room, and the first thing I see is an expansive ass in tight leggings. The woman's pulling a bucket and mop and using her fine ass to open the door. She's crouched over, her auburn hair tied in a high ponytail that sways over her shoulder, so I don't immediately see her face.

PROTECTING HIS SECRET BABY

But my heart rate quickens at the shape of her. The curvy figure, long neck, thick hair. Then she turns, and my heat skips a beat.

It's her. Jodie.

My Jodie.

Right here in the briefing room.

The room spins, and I think I'm going to fall. My attention zones in on her, my eyes hardly believing it's Jodie.

Her soft pink mouth is exactly as I remember it, with high, rosy cheekbones and hazel eyes that widen as she sees everyone staring at her.

My world spins. Time stands still.

It's her.

In the briefing room.

My feet have been resting on the chair in front of me, and they fall to the floor as I sit up in my seat. The noise makes her look up, and our eyes lock.

Her mouth pops open, her eyes widening in shock. The room fades away, and it's just the two of us for one long moment, staring at each other across the room.

Worry lines crease her brow that weren't there eighteen months ago. There're dark smudges under her eyes, and they no longer sparkle. Instead, her eyes look at me cool and glazed.

This is Jodie, but not the carefree girl I remember.

"And this is our new cleaner."

Bronn lifts a hand to indicate Jodie, and she breaks her gaze from mine. Swallowing hard, she takes a breath and looks around nervously.

"Sorry, I didn't know everyone was in here."

The briefing room is designed so you can't see into it, with tinted glass windows and a thick door. We deal with some confidential movements and need a secure area. She couldn't have known we were in here until she opened the door.

Bronn gives her a rare smile.

"Don't apologize." He turns to us. "Jodie will be here for a few hours every day to keep things clean for us. But don't make her job hard. Use the dishwasher and keep your desk tidy."

"I'll go start in the kitchen," she mutters.

Without looking at me, she wheels her cleaning cart out of the room, and the door swings shut behind her.

For the first time in eighteen months, deep in my belly, I feel a small flicker of hope.

4
JODIE

Holy shitballs. Kieren is working here.

The man who's been haunting my dreams, the man I never thought I'd see again is actually here in the same building as me.

In the long eighteen months since we met, I've imagined this moment many times. And in every scenario, I was cool as a cucumber and looking fabulous. I imagined thanking him for his service and then saying something smart and witty and dismissive before turning away.

In no scenario was I on my first cleaning job, looking like a hot mess from Layla keeping me up all night, and pushing a cleaning trolly.

My pulse is racing like it's in the Kentucky Derby as I push my cleaning trolling into the kitchen. Gripping the sides of the counter, I try to get my weak knees under control.

Damn that man. He looks as good as I remember. My body is heated all over, and there's a dampness pooling in my panties.

Grabbing a glass, I run a cool drink of water and gulp it

down. But it does nothing to quench the heat between my legs.

"Jodie."

Kieren's deep rumbling voice from the kitchen door makes my body tremble, and my knees almost give in.

With a deep breath, I turn around slowly, hoping he can't see the effect he's having on me.

"I've been looking for you," he says.

On closer inspection, Kieren looks rough. The thick hair I remember running my hands through is shaggy and peppered with silver. There're dark circles under his eyes, and he stinks like a brewery.

He's obviously still spending his nights drinking in bars and picking up women.

A prickle of disappointment starts at the base of my spine. I swallow it down, annoyed with myself.

What did I expect from a guy who I met in a bar?

I shrug my shoulders and hold my arms out.

"Here I am."

Kieren stares at me, his eyes unashamedly roving over my body, drinking me in. He looks as thirsty as a man lost in the desert.

"You left without leaving a note."

It takes me a moment to realize he's referring to the last morning of our hookup.

We spent an amazing weekend together, and on the final night, we slept together. It was my first time—my only time—though Kieren doesn't know that.

How could I tell a guy who picks women up at a bar that it meant so much more to me than the casual fling we agreed on? I got scared of my feelings for a man who was so obviously a player, so I left before he could leave me, leaving a scribbled note and no phone number.

But I can't tell him any of this.

I just shrug again. "It was a fling, Kieren. I barely remember it."

Oh god, I'm such a bad liar, but I keep my gaze steady and am satisfied to see his expression falter.

"It wasn't just a fling for me." He takes a step closer, and I back away from his intensity until my butt hits the counter. His look is so sincere that I almost believe him. But isn't that what players say when they want another hookup?

"I was deployed the day after you left. There was no way to reach you. You didn't leave a number."

It's true. I remember how powerful it felt to be the one to leave first, to walk out of his room while he was still asleep without leaving any way for him to contact me.

I regretted that bitterly a few weeks later.

"It was a long tour and my last one. I got back nine months ago and I've been looking for you ever since."

He takes my hands in his, and a jolt of warmth skips through my veins.

"You're all I've thought about. This is our chance, Jodie."

I try to look away, but I'm mesmerized by his intense gaze and the things he's saying and the way he's grasping my hands like his life depends on it.

I feel dizzy, and I'm not sure which way my heart is facing anymore. Every word Kieren says is what I dreamed he'd say to me, what I longed to hear during those long, lonely months when I found out Layla was on the way.

I went searching for Kieren. I tried to find him to tell him about the baby growing inside me. But his apartment was locked up, and no one answered the door any of the dozens of times I knocked.

His neighbors looked me up and down like I was trash asking about him. I assume he must have all sorts of discarded woman come looking for him. One neighbor took pity on me and told me Kieren had been deployed but no one knew where. I contacted the local Army base, but they wouldn't give me any information.

My anger grew inside me alongside my baby. I felt discarded. I felt like a fool. I knew it was just a hookup, but I still imagined Kieren turning up and telling me something different.

There were long, lonely nights when I cried, hugging my growing belly, imagining Kieren turning up and telling me everything was going to be okay.

But he never did.

I had my baby. I learned to get by on my own. I learned that men really are only after one thing, that you can't rely on them, and the only person you can rely on is yourself. And my sister.

I snatch my hands away from Kieren and force my voice into something light.

"It was a fling, Kieren, just a fun weekend. Thank you for that."

Hurt crosses his face. I guess I just shot down his hopes for another hookup.

Before I can lose my resolve, I push my cleaning cart out of the kitchen. I have a daughter to think about now, and I will not fall for the charms of an older ex-military hero again.

5
KIEREN

*M*y head's still spinning when I get home that afternoon. Closing the apartment door behind me, I lean against the cool wood, trying to get my thoughts in order.

After months of looking for Jodie, she turns up in my office.

I don't know where she's been hiding. I've scoured every bar on the Sunset Coast. And just like that, she turns up in my office.

She looked like I remembered her, thick hair swept off her face in a messy ponytail. I remember what it felt like to have that hair wrapped around my fist as I kissed her swollen lips.

The memory of Jodie's lips makes my dick twitch in my pants.

She was nervous in the bedroom, like a shy rabbit that I had to coax out of hiding, caressing her softly until she came apart under my touch, her body quivering against mine.

And when I entered her, it was pure bliss, her pussy so tight and hungry, her moans penetrating my nerve endings until I exploded underneath her, both of us climaxing too soon.

I thought we'd have time to make love again. I thought there'd be more opportunities to explore her body, to make her whine with pleasure the way she had when I first touched her.

But in the morning, Jodie was gone, and I was deployed the next day. There was no way to reach her, no chance to tell her how I felt.

Not that it matters if what she said in the kitchen is true.

She said it was just a fling, but I don't believe her. I felt the way her pulse jumped when I took her hands. I saw her pupils dilate.

She said it didn't mean anything to her. She's in denial. I'll make it mean something to her. I'll make it mean everything to her.

If Jodie just gives me one more chance, I'll prove to her what my heart already knows—we're meant to be together.

My throat is parched, and the hangover has subsided to a dull emptiness.

On autopilot, I open the fridge and reach for a beer. This is what I do. When the drink wears off and the emptiness slides in, I reach for a drink.

I pop open the bottle to a cold beer and bring it to my lips.

Then I remember Jodie's face in the kitchen, her critical look as she took in my disheveled appearance, the way she stepped away from me when I went toward her.

I'm not the man she met eighteen months ago. Back then I was holding back my demons by frequenting bars. I met her on a Friday night, and I didn't drink again until I realized she'd left on Sunday.

If I'm going to prove to Jodie that I'm her man, then I

need to clean myself up. I need to face my demons and get off the booze.

I take the beer bottle from my lips. The bitter smell is tempting, but not as tempting as being in the arms of Jodie.

Upending the bottle, I tip the contents down the sink. The stench of sour beer fills the kitchen and I nearly retch. The glugging noise feels like my insides are draining away.

I grab the other bottles from my fridge and drain those too. Then I take the half-finished bottle of bourbon from the cupboard and pour that after the beer.

It fizzes in the sink and gurgles down the drain, adding a sharp alcohol stench to my kitchen.

"Time to get some fresh air."

I change into my jogging shorts and slip on my running shoes. Dropping the empty bottles in my over-flowing recycling bin, I head out for my first jog in months.

With fresh air in my lungs and my head clearing, I breathe deeply, feeling better with ever step, feeling more alive.

If Jodie won't take me as I am, then I'll be a better man. I'll be the type of man she can be proud of. The type of man she deserves.

6
JODIE

I'm humming as I swipe my cloth over the kitchen bench in the Sunset Security kitchen. This has got to be the easiest gig. These guys are all ex-military and know how to keep things neat and tidy. I barely have to do anything.

My mind drifts, as it has so annoyingly been doing over the past week, to Kieren. He's kept out of my way or not been in the office over the last week, and I'm grateful for that.

And if I find myself spending a little extra time on my appearance in the mornings and making sure my clothes are at least not dirty or torn, then I tell myself it's because I want to make a good impression at work. It's definitely not for him.

It was a shock seeing Kieren again, and I'm not sure my body has totally relaxed yet. I remember his hands on me and the way his skilled fingers worked my pulsing core until I came undone.

The thought makes my body flush hot, and I pause in wiping the kitchen counter until my racing pulse gets under control.

The door to the kitchen opens, and my heart leaps into my throat. But it's not Kieren. It's Bronn. And I'm annoyed at how disappointed I feel by that.

"You do anything other than cleaning work?"

I've gotten used to Bronn's straight talking, and his lack of pleasantries doesn't faze me.

"I did some bar work once."

Bronn casts his eyes over me appraisingly but not in a creepy way. I get the feeling he's assessing me somehow.

I'm a big woman, tall and wide and a little round, even more so since having a kid. I stand up tall, proud of my five-foot-seven height.

"You ever do any security work?"

I'm not sure where this is going, and I'm not sure I like it.

"No…"

"You want to?"

I stare at him for a long moment. I know some men find my size intimidating, but I'm a big softy underneath. I'm not made to do security.

"I don't think so…"

"I'll pay you triple the cleaning rate."

Now he's got my attention. I'm on just above minimum wage, and that doesn't include what I have to fork out for the cleaning supplies. The extra money would be a godsend.

"It's a day's work at triple what we pay you now."

That would pay off the water bill and means I can do two hot showers a week for a while. And I'll be able to pick up a bit of meat this week to see if Layla likes chicken. Plus, I can put any extra aside for when Bertha does eventually go to car heaven, as I know she will.

It's too good to turn down, but I'm not qualified to be a security guard.

"What do I have to do?"

"You don't have to do anything. We've got a job with a minor politician, and she's insisting on having a woman on the team."

"Can't you ask Amy?" I think about the receptionist, the sweet but tough talking daughter of one of the scariest looking men who works here. She may be small, but with a dad like that, I bet she knows how to take down men twice her size.

"Amy's too petite looking. Security like this is all about show. You look the part."

I'm choosing to take that as a compliment. Looking intimidating is a good thing, right?

"I don't have any experience. What if something happens?"

"You'll be with one of our guys the whole time. If anything happens, which is unlikely, then he'll step in. You just need to be a presence, make her feel like we're listening to her wishes."

"What does it involve?"

"You'll be in the car that picks her up from the airport and delivers her to the venue. You'll walk her to the entrance and back to the car when she finishes. Other than that, it's a lot of waiting around in the car."

It sounds like an easy way to earn a quick buck. But I'm not sure if it'll fit in with Layla's schedule.

"What are the hours?"

Bronn cocks his head, probably wondering why I'm not biting his arm off for the opportunity.

"It's an easy day. Pick up is ten in the morning and you'll be done by three. I'll pay you for a full eight-hour day."

I'm about to say that won't be necessary, but I stop myself. This is easy money. I can't turn it down.

"Okay."

Bronn gives me a rare smile. "Good. You've got a good

physique for security and a sensible head on your shoulders. You should consider it."

Again, I think it's a compliment, which is rare coming from Bronn.

He turns to leave, but before he does, something occurs to me.

"Who's your guy on the job?"

Bronn turns back to me, and there's a flicker of a smile across his face before he arranges his features to neutral.

"Kieren will be on the job with you."

Kieren. Of course it's Kieren.

Bronn leaves the door swinging shut after him, and I wonder if he knows about our history. Is this some setup? Are Kieren's buddies trying to force us together?

I decide I don't care. I need the money for Layla, and if that means spending a day with Kieren, then that's what I'll have to do.

7
KIEREN

Light raindrops fall as I escort the client into the brown brick building where her meeting is taking place. On the other side of the woman is Jodie, her head bent inwards as the politician talks to her.

The white shirt of Jodie's security uniform shows her heavy breasts to perfection, the fabric sticking to her skin where the drops of rain land.

I try not to stare at her, but it's hard when she looks so damn good dressed up in a uniform. Whatever inspired Bronn to get her on the job, I'll never know, but I'm grateful. It makes me wonder if he knows about us, if Seth has told him anything. I decide I don't care. I get to spend the day with Jodie and that's all that matters.

One day to convince her that I'm the man she needs me to be.

The politician reaches the front door, and her aide opens it for her. It's a private residence, and we're not invited inside. Whatever threat we're protecting her from, real or perceived, hasn't materialized in the short drive from the airport to her meeting.

The woman talks quietly to Jodie, and I can't hear what they're saying, but Jodie responds with a flurry of hand activity and a furrowed brow. The aide holds an umbrella over the both of them while I stand by stoically in the rain and wonder what the hell they're talking about.

"Thank you for your insight," the politician says to Jodie, giving her arm a squeeze before disappearing into the house.

I look at Jodie with a raised eyebrow, but she only smiles mysteriously at me.

With the politician safely inside, we retreat to the waiting car. The rain falls heavier, and I jog ahead to open the car door for Jodie.

Once she's inside, I scoot around to the other side of the car and slide into the back seat next to her. It's a stretched limo that smells of expensive leather and good coffee, and we've got it to ourselves for the rest of the morning.

"So, what were you two chatting about?"

Jodie gives me a secretive smile. "Wouldn't you like to know?"

"Yes, I would. It might be important for security."

Jodie snort laughs, and I'm reminded of the carefree girl I met eighteen months ago.

"She was asking me how I felt about recent policy changes, wanted a laypersons point of view, I guess."

"She didn't ask me." I turn away, mock offended.

"No. I get the feeling she wanted a woman's opinion."

"And did you give her your opinion?"

"I certainly did."

I think about the heated look on Jodie's face and smile.

"I'm sure you did." I love the fact that Jodie's opinionated. It's what kept us up talking through the night on that first weekend together.

She smiles back at me, her eyes dancing.

I want to keep that look on her face, the carefree, challenging look that I fell in love with. I want to emulate that weekend, where we talked for hours, sharing our thoughts and opinions on everything apart from ourselves.

"So, what have you been doing with yourself for the last eighteen months?"

Jodie's face shuts down immediately, and she visibly seems to retreat. It's the wrong thing to say, and I don't know why.

"Not much," she mumbles, turning to look out the rain-stained window.

She's hiding something. I don't know what, but I'm determined to find out.

"You been back to the Sea Hopper?"

She shakes her head. "Not since…" Her sentence trails off as she shakes her head, lost in her own thoughts.

I get the feeling that weekend is painful for her somehow, which gives me hope in a sick way. Maybe it means she does care, that it did mean as much to her as it did to me.

"I've been back loads."

She looks around sharply, and a hint of jealousy flashes across her face before she turns back to the window.

I can't hide my satisfaction. She doesn't like the idea of me going out to bars. She probably thinks I've been picking up women, but that couldn't be further from the truth.

"I went back looking for you."

Jodie's gaze darts to mine, and there's a glimmer of hope in them. That look is all I need to keep going, to give me hope that I might be able to break down the wall she's constructed around herself to keep me out.

I sidle across the seat and hook my leg up so I'm facing her.

"I was deployed the day after we…" I was about to say hooked up, but that doesn't do justice to what I felt that weekend, to the connection we had. "The day after that weekend."

She looks up at me again, her hazel eyes round and wide.

"Thank you for your service. I'm not sure I ever said that to you before."

I wave a hand dismissively. I don't need her thanks. I should be the one thanking her.

"When I was over there, I knew it would be my last tour."

I look down at my hands, trying to find the words to explain what I felt, the crushing buildup in my chest of twenty years of service, the emptiness with every mission—with every kill.

When I first joined, I had a conscience. I used to feel things deeply. I remember my first kill. It threw me for weeks. I couldn't eat or sleep properly with the horror of what I'd done.

But by the last mission, I felt nothing, only a hollowness, an emptiness every time I pulled the trigger.

I was exactly what the Army needed me to be: a trained, heartless killer.

That's when I knew it was time to get out.

But I can't tell Jodie any of this. I can't let her see that dark part of my heart. All I can show her is how she healed me without even knowing.

When I look up again, she's watching me with compassion in her eyes as if she can see into my very soul.

"It got bad, this tour. I can't tell you details, but something went wrong, and it was a bad retreat."

I run a hand over my eyes. Our missions as a Special Forces team were dangerous, covert, ruthless.

I can't tell her what happened, and I don't want to anyway. Jodie doesn't need to know the details of what we do to keep this country safe.

"Every time I felt myself going to a dark place, do you know what I did?"

She shakes her head slightly.

"I thought about you. The way your eyes light up when you laugh, your hair spread out on my pillow, the scent of jasmine from the bodywash you use."

My hands take hers, and she doesn't pull away.

"I thought about your lips pressed to mine, the way your body felt against me."

Jodie's lips part, and her breathing gets heavy. I move forward, wanting, needing her to understand what she means to me.

"You're my guiding light, Jodie. You're what got me through the hard times. Just you."

8
JODIE

I'm struck dumb by the words coming out of Kieren's mouth. My heart yearns to accept them as truth, to believe that I mean something to this man, this wounded veteran who carries his scars on the inside, whose darkness lurks behind the smile of his eyes.

I remember seeing his darkness on that first weekend we spent together. I never told him, but he thrashed out in his sleep, chased by demons in the dead of night. Could it really be true that I mean something to him?

"I thought about how we stayed up talking 'til dawn, but most of all, I thought about how our bodies fit together."

His voice is mesmerizing, and he leans closer until I can smell his scent—musky bodywash and coffee. The scent memory is so powerful that heat pools in my belly, and I clench my thighs together.

"I thought about your breasts pressed against my chest…"

My eyes close as I let him carry me away on his memories. All thoughts flee my mind, and there's nothing but the soft caress of his hot breath against the skin of my neck.

"I thought about your legs wrapped around my waist…"

My nipples pebble, aching for him to caress me, aching to feel the touch I've yearned for.

"I thought about my cock sliding inside you…"

I let out an involuntary whimper as his soft lips whisper in my ear, the breath sending delicious shivers down my spine and causing a damp heat between my legs.

My chest is heaving as he presses his mouth to my throat, and a moan escapes my lips.

"I thought about moving inside you, and the little noises you make when you come…."

Kieren's hand slides up my leg. I should stop him. I should put an end to the madness that's taken me over. But my core's on fire, and instead of pushing Kieren away, I slide my hips forward on the seat, willing his hand to touch me between the legs, to press against my throbbing center.

"I thought about your sweet little pussy and what I'd do to it when I got home and found you again."

Gushes of heat flood my panties, and I push my hips upward to meet his hand. With smooth strokes, he rubs my needy pussy while his mouth devours my throat.

"Kieren…"

With his name on my lips, I surrender.

I surrender to the need I have to feel him touch me. I've dreamed about this for too long, and the reality of it is so much better.

His mouth finds mine as his hands slide down my pants, popping open the buttons of my fly. As we kiss, his fingers slip between my damp folds.

There's an urgency to his movements. I know we're on a job and anyone could open the door at any moment, but I don't care. I need this release.

It's been a long, lonely eighteen months. I've been exhausted and ready to give up. I've sat with a crying baby through the night. I've dealt with mastitis, a pregnancy-

PROTECTING HIS SECRET BABY

induced hernia. I've rushed Layla to the emergency room on three occasions, sure that her relentless cough was something worse. I've had baby vomit all over me and worse. And throughout it all, I've felt entirely and utterly alone.

Sure, my sister has been great when she could be, but she wasn't there through the long nights when a deep loneliness set in the pit of my stomach, a yearning to share the ups and downs with someone, a yearning to be taken care off.

I've imagined Kieren's hands on me too many times, but mostly I've been too exhausted to even give myself a release.

Now as he kisses me, I press my throbbing core into his palm, eighteen months of need and loneliness coming out in this one moment.

I'm panting hard and moaning with every stroke of his skilled fingers. I don't care about the noises I'm making. Kieren has unleashed something inside of me that's been pent up for too long.

Everything else flees from my mind. There is no baby to look after, no overdue bills to worry about, no cleaning jobs to do. For this moment only, there is just this incredible feeling emanating from my center that's taking over my whole body.

I grind onto Kieren's hand while his other hand gropes my breasts, tweaking my nipples and making me moan like a wild animal in heat.

"Kieren..."

I cry out his name as I explode, shards of sharp pleasure shooting through my body, my mind taken over by the sweet oblivion of pleasure.

The orgasm consumes me for a long, beautiful moment. The world is sweet, and there's nothing but my own body. I'm floating above myself as the release works its way through my veins. Slowly, the sounds of the outside world seep into my consciousness. I feel the cool leather seat under my bare bottom and hear the sound of rain tapping the windows.

When I open my eyes, Kieren is staring at me, looking as satisfied as I feel.

"I love you, Jodie."

That sobers me up pretty quickly. I sit up and adjust my uniform, pulling up my pants and doing up the buttons on my blouse that I don't remember undoing.

I can't process what he's saying. I can't look at him. Maybe he thinks he loves me, but we had one weekend together a year and a half ago. My life has changed since then.

"I'm not the same girl you met eighteen months ago."

He stops my hand and gently takes it in his. They're sticky from my juice coating his fingers, which makes it feel intimate. It's too special and close.

"Then let me get to know who you are now because I can guarantee that I'll love that Jodie too."

He has no idea what he's saying. If he knew about Layla, he wouldn't be so keen. No one wants to be an instant father, especially not a man who likes to frequent bars on weeknights.

"I don't think so."

I pull my hands away and finish doing up the buttons.

I feel like a proper bitch, but I've worked too hard to make things stable for Layla. I can't have Kieren messing with my emotions. I have to put her first, which means doing something really nasty to get him off my back.

"But we have a connection. I know you feel it."

"What I felt is a really good orgasm." I put on a big smile that I don't feel. "Thank you for that. You're as good as I remember."

Kieren stares at me, his head tilted like I'm some kind of

curious object he's analyzing. There's hurt in his eyes, and I hate myself for that.

"Is that all I am to you? Someone to make you come?"

Oh god, no. He's so much more than that. The father of my child. The man I've thought about every day and every lonely night since I met him. The man who I cried over endlessly when I tried to find him and found out he was gone. The man I swore to forget about and even did a cleansing ceremony to get him out of my head and heart. The man who, if I let him in even a little bit, will make me vulnerable and open to hurt. I can't go through Kieren breaking my heart a second time. Because I have a daughter to look after now, and she needs me to be whole and sane and not crying into my pillow.

"Yeah. That about sums it up."

Kieren's face falls, and I look away before tears spring to my eyes. I'm going to hell for doing this to him, but it's the right thing to do, isn't it?

At that moment, the walkie-talkie crackles, and we're told the client is ready to leave the building.

Without a glance back at Kieren, I get out of the car and slam the door behind me.

9
KIEREN

Touching my fingers to my nose, I breathe in deeply, and there it is. It's faint but still there—the musky scent of Jodie.

Seeing her lost in ecstasy and feeling her writhing on my hand made my balls pull up so tight I thought I was going to come in my pants.

Then when she told me I was nothing to her, I was devastated. Until I realized it's not true. It can't be true.

I saw the way she looked at me, the need in her eyes. It wasn't just for a release. I knew it when she mewled my name. It's me she needs, only me, even if she can't admit it yet.

Something's holding her back, something big.

Whatever it is, I can deal with it. I can support her in any way she needs.

Which is why I'm waiting for her when she starts her shift the next day.

I watch her get out of her beat-up car through the kitchen window. That thing can't be safe on the road. The first thing we're doing is getting her a new car.

PROTECTING HIS SECRET BABY

She struggles getting her cleaning gear out of the trunk, and I scramble to help her. By the time I've gotten into the parking lot, she's hauling her cleaning bucket to the door.

"Let me help you with that."

I take the bucket from her, and she mutters a thanks.

But before we go inside, I turn and block the door.

"Jodie. I don't know what it is that's happened and why you keep pushing me away…."

She folds her arms, giving me a hard look. Any other man would probably take the hint, but I've waited too long for this. I'm not giving up without a fight.

"Whatever it is, we can face it together."

She gives a snort and looks away. I get the feeling that I've let her down in some way, but I don't know how. She's the one that left with only a note. If anything, I should be mad, but I'm not.

"If you're struggling…."—I indicate her car—"I can help. You don't have to worry about money again. You don't have to clean for a job. I'll take care of you. I'll buy you any car you want."

I mean it. I'll look after this woman for the rest of my days. I'll give her everything she needs.

When she looks back at me, her eyes are fiery, and I have an uneasy feeling I've said the wrong thing.

"You want to buy me now? And what do you expect in return?"

Ah shit. I definitely said the wrong thing. "That's not what I meant…"

But the damage is done. I don't know how I'm doing it, but every time I see this woman, instead of winning her over, I just make it worse.

"I just mean that I'm here for you, whatever you need."

"You gave me what I needed yesterday, Kieren."

The words sting. I guess that's what she wanted.

I stand aside and let her into the building, wondering how the hell I've managed to fuck it up so bad.

A car door slamming draws my attention to Seth crossing the parking lot. He's got a rueful look on his face like he knows exactly what's just gone on.

"I can look into it, buddy, find out what's going on with her. Then you'll know what it is, and you can stop being such a fuck-up."

It's tempting. But I won't do it to Jodie.

"No thanks, man. I'm not snooping on her."

Or not much anyway. Leo's got a talent for winning people over, and I've already asked him to sweet-talk Jodie's address out of Amy.

If she won't tell me what's going on, I'll got to her house and find out.

10
JODIE

I've been agitated all day since my run in with Kieren. Pushing him away felt like the right thing to do, but my stomach's been in knots and my chest feels heavy.

Layla must have sensed my agitation because it took a long time for her to settle. I've finally got her down when the doorbell goes.

Layla's eyes flick open, and she holds out a tubby fist.

"Who the hell comes calling during bedtime?" I mutter to myself. Obviously, someone who doesn't have kids.

I pat her blanket down soothingly.

"I'll just see who that is, sweetie. You get some sleep."

I leave her gurgling to herself as I sneak quickly across the living room to the front door, hoping she can lull herself to sleep.

If she doesn't get to sleep, I'm going to murder whoever's on the other side of this door.

Pulling the door open a crack, my heart leaps into my throat when I see Kieren.

Despite myself, I feel a surge of warmth at his persistence. This guy doesn't give up. Then I remember it's because he doesn't know about Layla. It's easy to be persistent when you don't know there's a baby involved.

I step out onto the doorstep and pull the door closed behind me.

"How did you know where I live?"

Him turning up here is a bad idea. I only hope that Layla has taken herself off to sleep. I'm not ready to explain to him about her yet. I know that no matter what happens between us, he has a right to know about his daughter, but that will happen when I'm ready, when I can control my feelings around him. And that is definitely not tonight.

He indicates the parking lot. "It was easy to spot your vintage car."

I can't help my smile. Calling Bertha vintage is a polite way of saying she'd too old to be on the road.

Kieren must see my look as an invitation because he pulls a bunch of flowers from behind his back.

"Peace offering."

They're deep purple tulips, my favorite type of flower, and I feel my resolve slipping.

Kieren looks so contrite standing on the doorstep. How easy it would be to invite him in, to let him into my heart.

But that only leads to pain.

I hesitate, not sure if I should take the flowers or not. He'll read too much into it if I do. There's a loud wail from inside, the distinctive cry of a baby. My eyes dart to Kieren, and I catch the look as his eyes widen.

The wail turns to a steady cry, and I watch his reaction as realization sets in.

"You have a baby?"

"Yeah." I nod.

PROTECTING HIS SECRET BABY

For once, he's too stunned to speak. "Is that why you've been brushing me off?"

I look at him long and hard.

Do I tell him? Do I tell Kieren he has a daughter? Would he run, or would he stay?

He's a player. I met him at a bar. He won't want to be saddled with a baby. I can't tell him. Not yet.

When I first found out Layla was on the way, I hunted for Kieren. I tried to find him, convinced he would step up and do the right thing. But after eighteen months on my own, I've found my own way. Me and Layla have our own routines, and we're fine without him.

No, I don't need him disrupting our lives.

The cry gets louder, and Kieren shifts uncomfortably.

"Do you need to go see what it—ah, he, she wants?"

I pull the door open a crack.

"I do. Before she wakes my boyfriend," I say quickly.

Kieren does a double take. I hate myself for the lie that rolls easily off my tongue. But I can't do this right now. I can't tell him the truth.

"You're with someone?"

"Yes, Kieren. Babies have fathers, you know."

He looks shell-shocked. His hair falls messily over his eyes, and I long to tuck it behind his ear, to pull him close. But I can't. I must be firm.

"But the other day…?"

"Was nice. But it can't happen again."

Kieren's still looking shocked as I duck inside the house.

"So, thank you for your concern, but we're all doing just fine."

As I close the door on him, my last impression is of Kieren with a broken look on his face, the bunch of tulips hanging by his side.

I lean with my back against the door for a moment,

wondering if I've done the right thing, feeling regret for all that happened and all that could have been.

Then Layla wails again, and I go to her.

Regret is an indulgence I don't have time for. I have a child to take care of.

11
KIEREN

My body sways drunkenly to Aerosmith's "Don't Want to Miss a Thing" coming from the jukebox. It takes a few beats for my head to catch up to my body, the liquor making me slow. Slow and numb. Exactly how I want to be.

In no scenario did I envision Jodie having a baby and a boyfriend. I was so caught up in my own memories of our perfect weekend together and the electric connection I thought we had. I was sure she'd felt it too. Or at least felt it enough not to immediately find someone else, someone she wanted to have a baby with.

The thought of Jodie with someone else sends a blood-boiling shot of jealousy through my veins. Even through my alcohol-addled body, I still feel a possessiveness for her.

I pick up my bourbon glass and drain it, welcoming the sweet oblivion that can't come soon enough.

Through blurry vision, I see a woman coming toward me. She's too short but her face looks pleasant enough and kind of familiar, but I can't see her features properly through the alcohol blur. Maybe this is what I need, a new kind of way to forget about Jodie.

"Hey, beautiful. What's your name?"

The woman tilts her head and gives me a pitying look that's not unkind.

"Don't try it, Kieren. I'm not your type."

Confusion floods my brain as I feel strong arms wrap around me from behind.

"I'll let you get away with that because you're drunk, but you come onto my woman again, I will kill you."

Seth's familiar voice hums in my ear, although he's usually not so tough talking.

Then I remember why I recognize the woman. It's Kayla, Seth's new girlfriend. I giggle because the last thing I would ever do is come onto a buddy's woman.

"You two here for a drink?"

"Time to go."

Seth loosens his grip on me but keeps a firm hold of my shoulder. He pulls me toward the door, and I stumble over my feet.

"But we haven't done tequila shots."

Seth's grip is firm and unrelenting. He can be a tough bastard when he wants to be. "No shots tonight, Kieren. We're taking you home."

His tone is no nonsense, and I look to Kayla for help, hoping to find an ally. But she just shakes her head at me.

"I'll drive your car back to our place," she says. "You can crash in the spare room. I'll make you a grilled cheese when we get in."

Kayla's expression is kind, and I can see why Seth is crazy about her. Compared to his stern demeanor, she's a sight for sore eyes.

"You're sweet."

Seth growls, and I giggle again.

"In a platonic way, dude. I'm not hitting on your girl."

Seth manages to wrangle me out of the bar and into his car. The ride home makes me feel nauseous, and it takes a few minutes of sitting in the cool night air before I can make it into the house.

As promised, Kayla makes me a grilled cheese sandwich, then takes herself off to bed. Seth's made coffee, and by the way he's waiting for me at the dining table, I can tell he wants to talk.

I feel like a wayward teenager getting growled at by his dad. On top of everything that's happened today, the last thing I need is a fucking lecture from my best friend. I know my behavior was appalling. I don't need anyone else to tell me that.

"I'm not in the mood for a lecture, Seth. I just found out she's got a fucking boyfriend and a baby."

Seth holds his hand up, and his expression softens.

"I'm not going to give you a lecture, Kieren. If you want to fuck your liver up, that's up to you."

He indicates a chair and I sink into it. Seth takes a sip of coffee while I nibble on the grilled cheese.

"Hmm. She's a good cook. Kayla."

That gets a smile out of Seth. "Yeah, a real gourmet."

I take sip of coffee, and the hot liquid almost scalds my tongue.

"She doesn't have a boyfriend," Seth says.

I pause with the sandwich halfway to my mouth. "What are you talking about?"

"I know you don't want to spy on her or anything, but I did some digging anyway. There are some things you should know."

The alcohol faze leaves my head as I try to piece together what Seth is saying. It's wrong to dig up info on Jodie the way that Seth's doing it. He did some dodgy stuff to win

Kayla over. I love the guy like a brother, but I'm not going to be that man.

Yet… I'm curious as hell.

"How do you know she doesn't have a boyfriend? She's got a baby."

"Yes." Seth clasps his hands together. "She does have a baby. That is true. But there's no boyfriend."

"So, she made that bit up? Why would she do that?"

It doesn't make me feel any better. Jodie's so repulsed by me that she invented a boyfriend to get rid of me.

"Don't worry about the boyfriend or lack thereof." Seth leans forward and talks slowly as if he's trying to explain something to a five-year-old.

"The key here is the baby."

I don't know what he's getting at. The fact that Jodie is a solo mum doesn't make me feel much better.

Some scumbag has left her alone, left her by herself to raise their kid.

At least I can step up for her. I can be the man she needs, the father to her baby, and the man to take care of both of them. If she'll have me.

"I don't mind raising someone else's kid if that's what Jodie needs from me."

Seth gives me a look like I'm stupid. Maybe I am, but hell, I'll do anything for that woman.

"The baby is nine months old."

He says it slowly and deliberately like there's some significance in that. But the lasting alcohol in my brain can't quite piece it together.

So, she had a kid nine months ago. That would have been about nine months after our weekend together…

Holy shit.

The realization hits me like a bowling ball to the stomach, and I'm suddenly stone-cold sober.

"It's mine, isn't it?"

I know as soon as the words leave my mouth that it's the truth.

My baby. Mine and Jodie's. I'm the scumbag that left her to have a baby on her own, to raise it on her own. She probably came looking for me when she found out she was pregnant, but I was deployed.

No wonder she hates me.

Seth nods slowly, probably relieved to see his dumb-ass friend finally figured it out. "I can't be a hundred percent sure because she didn't put a name on the birth certificate, but the dates add up."

"Fuck."

I push the chair back and pace the room.

Seth's watching me carefully, probably worried I'm going to freak out and bust his house up or something stupid.

But all I can think about is the fact that I'm a father. I'm a father with the woman I love.

"This is fucking awesome."

Seth visibly relaxes.

"It might not be yours, but the dates check out."

"Oh, it's mine."

I fucking know it. In the heat of the moment, we never used a condom. I remember Jodie's fumbling hands on my cock. She was inexperienced, maybe even a virgin. There's no way she was doing what we did with other guys. I know it. I know it in my heart that the baby is mine.

I grab my keys off the table and head out of the room.

"Whoa, where you going?"

Seth catches my shoulder.

"I'm going to claim my family."

He gives me the patient dad look again.

"It's two in the morning and you stink like a brewery. I'm

not letting you drive, and you're not doing yourself any favors going around there now anyway."

He's right, as always.

"Fine. I'll stay here tonight, but tomorrow, when I'm clean and un-stinky, I'm going to get my family back."

12
JODIE

*I*t's lucky that Layla is an early riser because someone's banging on my door at seven in the morning.

I carry her, bouncing on my hip, to the front door, wondering who the hell thinks it's okay to knock on a door so early.

Kieren. That's who.

He's unshaven and his hair is a mess, but there's a new spark in his eyes when he sees me. Then his eyes travel to Layla, and he looks at her long and hard, delight and curiosity dancing across his face.

"She's mine, isn't she?"

My stomach lurches. He knows. Somehow, he knows.

There's excitement in his voice, and the way he's looking at her makes it impossible to deny his rights as a father.

I bite my lower lip and suck in my breath as I prepare to tell him the truth.

"Yes."

It feels good to say it. My chest feels lighter. "Yes, Kieren. Layla is your daughter."

The grin that spreads across his face is a wonderful sight to see. I suddenly realize how stupid it was not to tell him, to deny him the opportunity to know his daughter.

"Layla," he says slowly. "It's a nice name."

His gaze goes back to mine, and there's such wonder in his look that I feel my heart softening.

"I'm so sorry I wasn't here for you, Jodie. No wonder you hate me."

Something inside me melts at the words. Maybe that's all I needed to hear, an apology for something that I know couldn't be helped.

"I don't hate you, Kieren." Because the opposite is true. I love him. I've loved him since that amazing weekend we spent together.

"Can I come in?"

I hesitate. Telling him the truth about Layla is one thing. Inviting him into my life is quite another.

"I know there's no boyfriend." My cheeks turn crimson at the reminder of the lie I told him last night.

"But I know why you said it. I just want to meet my daughter."

He looks so sincere that I feel my defenses crumbling. What can it hurt for him to come in for coffee and spend some time with Layla? Whatever happens between us, he has rights as her father.

I open the door, and he follows me into the living room. Baby toys are scattered everywhere, and the smell of her nighttime diaper hangs in the air.

Kieren's nose wrinkles up at the smell, making me chuckle. "Welcome to parenthood."

I put Layla down on one of her play rugs, and she rolls onto her tummy, trying to pull herself up. She's so close to crawling. I know it'll happen any day soon.

"You want some coffee?"

The kitchen's connected to the living room, and I leave the two of them to get acquainted while I make the coffee.

My emotions are churning inside me as I watch him wiggle toys in front of her. Just watching him with Layla, his wonderous look, shows me what a good dad he could be.

I bring the hot drinks through and set them on the coffee table. Kieren sits next to me on the couch, leaving Layla wriggling on her playmat. She's shaking a rattle and laughing at the way the colored baubles inside move about.

"Jodie…" Kieren turns to face me and takes my hands in his. The warmth feels so good, so comforting. This time, I don't pull away.

"I'm so sorry I wasn't there for you, that you had to do this alone."

His voice is heavy with regret and pain, and the words wear away at the hard layer around my heart.

"But you're not alone anymore. I'll be here in whatever way you need me to be. As a father, as your man. Hopefully both. Whatever you need from me."

The words are nice to hear, but does he really know what he's getting into?

"You're not freaked out by being an instant dad?

He looks at Layla, and she gurgles a smile at him.

"No way. It's the best news I've had. I want to take care of you both, look after you."

I love what he's saying, but I have to be sure.

"Are you sure, Kieren? Because I can't have you in and out of my life. I need to put Layla first, and I need to know that if you're gonna be my man, you're not going to come and go."

His expression never leaves mine as he slides off the couch and onto one knee.

"If this is what it takes to show you how serious I am, then I'll do it."

SADIE KING

My heart leaps to my throat. He can't possibly be doing what I think he's doing.

"You can't be serious?"

"I've never been more serious in my life. You're all I've thought about since the moment I met you. You kept me sane in the dark times. You're the light that guided me out of the darkness. I love you, Jodie, and I'll love you and look after you and our children for the rest of my days. Will you marry me, Jodie?"

His hands are warm in mine, and as I look into his eyes, I feel the truth of his words.

I was so scared he wouldn't want us, but the opposite is true. He wants me and Layla. He wants the whole package.

My heart melts, the final barrier sliding away. My chest opens, and I feel lighter than I have in months, lighter than I have since that perfect weekend together.

"Yes." I don't even have to think about it. The words slip out. "Yes, yes, yes. I'll marry you."

Kieren grabs me around the waist, and I pull him onto me and then we're rolling on the couch as he plants kisses all over me.

"I love you, Jodie."

My body heats and there's a surge of dampness at the weight of him on top of me.

Layla giggles, thinking it's a game, and I'm brought back to reality.

Pushing Kieren off me, I scoop up my baby girl.

"We can't do that in front of the baby."

Kieren stands up, and his erection sticks out from his pants. "Do what?"

I giggle at the boner sticking out in his pants, and he gives me a mischievous grin.

"When does daycare open?"

I give him a playful punch on the arm.

"I can't just drop her in daycare because you want to…"

He cuts my words off with a slap to my butt that makes me jump and sends shocks of electric pleasure down my body.

"Maybe this once…"

Kieren plants a kiss on the nape of my neck.

"Good. Ger her ready. I'll meet you at my place."

He heads for the door, and I call after him.

"Hey, where you going?"

He gives me a secretive look. "I have to pick something up."

I don't know what he's up to, but I don't care. I twirl Layla around in my arms, and she giggles, wondering what's got her mommy so excited.

"We're going to be a family, sweetie. A real family."

13
KIEREN

As soon as I see Jodie's car pull up, I throw open the door to my apartment, too eager to wait for her to get up the stairs. My balls are pulled up tight, and my dick hasn't stopped being hard since she said yes and rolled with me on the couch.

Now it's time to claim my woman.

"Hey," she chirps happily as she sees me coming toward her. My hands go around her waist, and she squeals as I lift her into the air and carry her the rest of the way inside.

I've waited for this moment for eighteen months. I'm not waiting a second longer.

My foot pushes the door shut as I press Jodie up against the wall of the entryway, my lips crushing against hers.

Jodie moans underneath me, her breasts pushing against my chest like two glorious soft cushions.

My hands slide up her pert butt and around to the side of her hips. My hands can't get enough of her. It's like I have to feel every curve, every crevasse of her body. My fingers dig into the fabric of her leggings, kneading the flesh underneath.

My mouth devours her, the scent of jasmines making me woozy, making me lose myself in this moment—in this woman.

I will myself to slow down or else I'm going to lose it before we've even started. Pulling her head back, I look into her eyes. They're blazing with a heat as fiery as mine.

"I love you, Jodie."

Her pupils dilate at the words, then she says them back to me and my heart melts.

"I love you, Kieren."

We keep our eyes locked for a long moment. The love flowing between us is a soothing balm to my soul.

I feel the darkness receding just by being in the presence on this woman. And I marvel at the power of love.

I make a silent pledge that I will step up for Jodie and Layla. I'll be the man they need me to be, whatever it takes.

Jodie's hips move against me, and my cock gives an aching tug, reminding me of his needs.

I don't want the start of our life together to be consummated against a wall, no matter how much she grinds against me.

"Come with me."

Taking her hand, I lead Jodie into the bedroom and push her gently onto the satin sheets. She starts wiggling out of her leggings, but I stop her hands.

"I want to unwrap you."

I want to unwrap her every single day of my life. She's the perfect gift. My heart knows it and my body knows it, judging by the precum that seeps out as soon as my hands touch her silky thighs.

I try to go slow. But help me, God. It's hard when you've got a goddess before you.

I start gently, tugging her clothes of, but as every section of pale skin is exposed, each delicate sliver of her flesh sends a new heat coursing through me, causing my dick to throb and my heart to drum so hard I think my chest is going to burst open.

By the time we're naked, I'm like a wild animal possessed, nipping and sucking her gorgeous body, responding to her moans as I touch and lick and suck every inch of her.

When my tongue reaches her sex, Jodie arches her back, a desperate mewl escaping her lips. I nearly lose it right then and there. She's fucking perfect, and I never want her to stop making those noises.

Perspiration gathers in her naval, and I run my hands over her slick body, giving her all the attention she needs as my mouth works her core.

"Kieren…" she cries out as she comes, her orgasm shooting her juice into my mouth. It's the sweetest nectar I've ever tasted.

Licking her juices off my lips, I sit back and watch this beauty panting and writhing for more.

Her eyes are hooded as I slide my dick between her swollen pussy folds. I need to be inside her. I need it so bad.

"Kieren…" She's panting as she sits up on her elbows. "The first time that weekend… I was a virgin."

Ah shit. She trusted me enough to let me take her cherry and then I wasn't around when she needed me. A surge of regret shakes through me. Regret for the wasted months when we weren't together. Regret for all the ways I let her down by not being there.

"I'm so sorry, baby."

Jodie sits up and runs a hand up my arm.

"You have nothing to be sorry for. This is a new start. This is the start of us."

Her hands strokes my arm, moving to my navel and the length of my shaft.

PROTECTING HIS SECRET BABY

"I haven't been with anyone else since, and I never will. I'm yours, Kieren. I've only ever been yours."

She takes my shaft in both hands and guides me to the opening of her channel, and willingly, I go.

"I'm all yours, Kieren." She moans the words as my cock parts her swollen lips.

"And I'm yours."

Our gaze finds each other as I slowly thrust into her. Her eyes widen, but she keeps them locked on mine. And in that look, so much passes between us. I feel the connection, the love, the hope. This really is a new start, and this time, I won't let her down.

Her hips move to the rhythm, and her eyes droop closed.

"Keep your eyes on me," I command. "I want to see you come."

Her eyelids flicker open. Her lips part. My balls are pulled up tight, ready to unload, and I'm only holding on because I want her to come again.

My hands clutch her hips and her legs wrap around me, but we keep our eyes locked as the thrusting becomes faster, harder.

Then she's crying out my name, her pussy convulsing, her face scrunched up in ecstasy. It's the look of wonder in her eyes that pushes me over the edge.

I explode into her, shooting out the pent-up frustration from the last eighteen months, giving her everything I have and hoping it's enough.

We cling to each other, our bodies slick with sweat and trembling, our eyes locked until the quivering finally subsides and we collapse onto the bed.

We lie together, face to face, our noses almost touching. Jodie smiles a sleepy smile, and her eyes dance in the carefree way I remember.

My heart is full, my body spent, and my soul feels, for the first time in months, content, calm, and stable. No longer in darkness but held in the light, the light that can only come from love.

EPILOGUE

KIEREN

Seven years later…

The high-pitched notes of some boy band play out of the jukebox, and I wince at the screechy tones and cheesy lines.

On the barstool next to me, Jodie wiggles her hips in time to the music, her leg jiggling and her mouth humming the words between sips of her virgin Seabreeze.

"If you want to dance to this, then I will. That's how much I love you."

She shakes her head emphatically. "Oh no. I only know it because they play it at Layla's Jump Jam class."

That's where we are now, making musical choices based on what our kids want to listen to. I can't remember the last time I put on music that I wanted to listen to. Well, time to change that.

I set my non-alcoholic beer on the table and stride to the jukebox. It's full of tunes I don't recognize, and I have to flick through to a disc labeled *American Classics* before I find what I'm looking for.

"Learn to Fly" by the Foo Fighters, the first song Jodie and I danced to and the perfect tune to play on our anniversary.

As the generic pop tunes are replaced by grunty guitar, I get withering looks from the other patrons who don't look like they're old enough to shave, let alone drink.

But I don't give a shit. The only thing I care about in this moment is dancing with my wife.

"Come here."

I curl up a finger, beckoning Jodie onto the dance floor. She gives me a shy smile, playing coy like that first time I met her.

Her face carries more laughter lines these days, but she still has the power to take my breath away.

Jodie sets down her drink and sashays onto the dance floor.

I pull her close to me, and the scent of jasmine and baby milk fills my senses—the scent of home.

"Happy anniversary, baby," I murmur into her ear.

I take her hand in mine, and the other I slide around her waist. It glides over the soft cotton fabric of her summer dress.

It's not a song for slow dancing, but we make it into one, swaying to the music with our bodies pressed firmly together.

I can feel the outline of her thighs through her thin cotton dress, and it makes the blood rush through my body straight to my dick.

A gentle press of her hips lets me know that she feels my stiffness against her. After seven years of marriage, my wife still has the ability to make me instantly hard.

I guess our growing family is a testament to that.

Since Layla, we've had two more children, and there's another one on the way that we've only just found out about.

They're all girls so far. I'm woefully outnumbered, and I wouldn't have it any other way.

My girls are the light of my life, my reason for living.

They're the reason I haven't drunk a drop of alcohol in seven years. They're the reason I go to the gym three times a week to keep myself fit and healthy for them.

They're the reason I came clean to Bronn about the problems I'd been having since leaving the military. And they're the reason I took his recommendation for a counselor to help me work through the darkness that plagues too many returning servicemen and women.

My girls are the reason I'm still alive, and I'm thankful for them every single day.

But most off all, I'm thankful for Jodie, the light, the beacon that holds our family together and steers us through the rough days to calmer waters.

I press her cheek to mine as we move around the dance floor. I'm trying to ignore the way my feet stick to the plywood floor, the smell of stale beer that assaults my nostrils, and the sullen looks from the young clientele that clearly have no musical taste.

It started as a tradition, coming back to the Sea Hopper every year on our anniversary, the place where it all began so many years ago.

But it's clear with each passing year how much we've outgrown it.

Jodie lifts her sparkling eyes up to mine, and I can tell she's thinking the same thing.

"Should we get out of here?"

I nod. "Oh yeah. You want to go somewhere else? Get a dessert?"

We had dinner at a restaurant in town earlier. Jodie's sister is babysitting the kids, and she said to stay out as late as we want.

It's not even ten, yet I'm restless to get home. I can't explain it. But home is my happy place. where all the good things in my life are.

"I kinda miss the kids." Jodie whispers it like it's a secret, but I get it.

"So do I."

"Should we go home?"

Her eyes look hopeful, and as she says it, her hips bump against mine. There's a slight pressure, and she lowers her eyelashes.

It's a promise. The kids are at home, but so is our king-size bed with the satin sheets that glide over our naked bodies and the ensuite shower where we've made love countless times.

Oh yeah. I want to go home, all right. I want to check on my kids and give them a kiss as they sleep, then go upstairs and make love to my wife.

I take her hand and, without a backward glance at the bar, lead my wife home.

* * *

WHAT TO READ NEXT

PROTECTING HIS BEST FRIEND'S DAUGHTER

Twenty years of military discipline hasn't prepared me for one weekend with Amy...

Leo

Amy's the perfect woman. Sweet, funny, and curves that make my mouth water. Too bad she's my best friend's daughter and completely off-limits.

When he asks me to protect her, he has no idea how far I'll go to keep her safe.

Amy may be forbidden to me, but I won't let any other man touch her.

Amy

It's only ever been Leo. Since he made me laugh when I was twelve years old, I've had a crush on him.

But he still sees me as a little girl.

When we're thrown together for the weekend, it's my

chance to show him I'm more than a little girl. I'm a woman —his woman.

He thinks we should do the right thing. He thinks we can't be together.

Leo has a will of steel, and I'm determined to break him...

Protecting His Best Friend's Daughter is a forbidden love, age gap, romance featuring an OTT ex-military hero and the curvy woman he claims as his own.

Keep reading for an exclusive excerpt or get your copy from: mybook.to/SSProtectingHisBestFriendsDaughter

PROTECTING HIS BEST FRIEND'S DAUGHTER

CHAPTER ONE

Amy

At the sound of the door sliding open, I look up from the computer. As the receptionist for Sunset Security, it's my job to greet new clients with a sunny smile and pleasant demeanor. But the smile freezes on my lips when I see who it is coming in the main entrance.

"I bought you a cappuccino." The boy holds up a takeout cup with coffee that I didn't ask for and probably won't drink.

I've got a reusable takeout mug sitting under the desk that I use whenever I want coffee from the cafe next door, which is hardly ever since Bronn got the good coffee machine installed in the kitchen.

But since the one time I bought a cappuccino from the shop next door, this boy's got it in his head that he's doing something nice for me by bringing over a free drink every day.

It would be sweet if it wasn't such an obvious excuse to stare at my boobs.

"Thank you."

I've been brought up too polite to refuse a gift, so I thank him and take the drink, which sloshes over the rim and burns my fingers.

The boy—I forget his name. James or Jaxon or Jamie? I don't want to ask because it would be rude considering he's been coming in here for the last two weeks. Whatever his name is, he leans on the reception desk and gives me a nervous smile.

"I, um…"

His eyes flick to my chest, making me wish I'd worn a high-neck blouse instead of the low-cut one I put on trying to get someone else's attention.

When his gaze comes back to mine, his pimply cheeks are tinged pink.

At least he has the decency to be embarrassed about getting caught staring at my chest.

"I, um… Do you want to have a coffee with me sometime?"

He's nervous and sweet, and his brown eyes look both terrified and hopeful.

He's not bad looking, if you like that kind of thing, with a thick head of sandy hair and clear, youthful skin. His face is clean shaven and smooth. There're no scars of experience or lines on his face.

He's probably the same age as me, nineteen, or maybe a bit older.

I can hear my best friend Sarah's words in my head: *You're never gonna lose your v-card if you don't go on any dates.*

She's right. I should say yes. I should at least have coffee with this boy.

He smiles hopefully, and his eyes dart back to my breasts. His tongue flicks over his lips and this time he doesn't bother to look back up at my face.

I should. But there's only one man I'm interested in dating, and it's certainly not this boob-obsessed adolescent.

"Sorry." I give him what I hope is a reluctant smile. "I'm not allowed to date."

His gaze darts up to mine, and his brow furrows in confusion.

It's kind of true. My dad is always joking that I'm not allowed to go out with any boys. He banned me from dating when I was younger, but since I turned eighteen, he has no right to stop me. But the truth is, there's only one man I want to date, and he's not interested in me at all.

"How old are you?" the boy asks.

"I'm nineteen."

He looks concerned. "You should be able to make your own decisions."

He's getting indignant on my behalf, and it's kinda sweet but awkward. I was hoping he'd get the hint without me having to spell it out.

I shrug, which is the wrong move because his wandering eyes lock on my wobbling boobs. Ah, the pleasures of being a curvy girl. Every movement I make takes my boobs a few seconds to catch up.

"My dad's pretty tough. Ex-military, Special Forces."

The boy stands up straight, getting his elbows off my reception desk and his eyes off my tits.

"He doesn't let you date? Can't you go out anyway? You're an adult."

This boy's sweet, and maybe what I'm about to do is a little mean, but I hate saying a flat-out no. Besides, maybe it will scare him away for good and I won't have to put up with his boob staring anymore.

"I went on a date once without him knowing," I lie. "He tracked us down. Broke both the guy's arms."

The boy goes pale, and I try not to smile. "Broke his arms?" he asks faintly.

"Oh, don't worry." I'm really getting into this now. "They reckon he'll be out of hospital in a few more months."

The boy backs away from the reception desk looking horrified.

At that moment, the door that leads through to the office opens, and Leo strides through.

My pulse jumps up a notch at the sight of him. His weathered features and salt-and-pepper hair. The scar that runs behind his ear to halfway down his neck. The tattoos that snake down his thick, muscular arms, telling the story of his life.

Leo's gaze finds mine, a slight smile on his lips that disappears when he sees the boy, who has made the mistake of stealing another look at my chest.

"What the fuck are you staring at?"

Leo strides toward him and the boy stumbles backward, a look of pure terror on his face.

"I was… I was…"

Leo doesn't give him time to explain.

"You keep your eyes on me, kid, or on the floor."

The boy is shaking so hard I think he's going to wet himself.

"I was just bringing her some coffee, that's all. Don't break my arms, please."

Leo pauses and casts a look over his shoulder at me. His eyebrows shoot up in a questioning look.

Leo's blocking the boy's view of me so he can't see me trying not to crack up. I give my shoulders a little shrug, and Leo's eyes glint with mischief.

Then he puts his hard-ass Army face on and turns back to the boy.

"I don't want to see you in here again. If Amy wants a

coffee, I'll fetch it for her. You stay the fuck away from her. You understand?"

"Yes, sir." The kid trembles and I kind of feel sorry for him, but then I remember the uncomfortable feeling of his eyes on my boobs and all sympathy vanishes. Besides, I'm too busy enjoying the way Leo's back ripples with tension.

"Now get the fuck out of here."

He takes a step back, giving the kid enough room to scramble out of the door.

When Leo turns around, I burst out laughing. He shakes his head at me as he saunters over to the reception desk.

"Break his arms? What was that all about?"

I tell him about the story I concocted about my dad and how he must have assumed Leo was my father.

Leo grins, and by the time I've finished telling him the story, we're both laughing so hard my side hurts. I always end up laughing when I'm with Leo. He has a way of making me feel good whenever he's around.

"Good story, kid."

He ruffles my hair, and the good feeling inside me vanishes.

That's all I am to Leo. A kid.

He still thinks of me as a girl. He hasn't noticed that I've grown into a woman.

I've been in love with my father's best friend ever since I was twelve years old.

Dad was back from tour, and him and Mom were arguing again. Only this time, the arguing was quiet, which was worse than the shouting. I heard Mom use the word divorce, and I ran outside, too scared to hear any more.

I ran out to the treehouse and climbed inside. There were some loose boards in the ceiling, and I pulled them aside and pulled myself up onto the roof, hidden by the foliage of the maple tree.

I stayed there until the light faded and didn't come down even when they were calling my name.

It was Leo who found me huddled in the tree, shivering in the cool evening air.

He climbed up and sat with me, taking off his jacket to drape it over my shoulders.

At first neither of us spoke. He just sat with me until the light completely faded from the sky. Then he started telling me jokes. Bad, cheesy jokes, but they made me laugh.

He told me funny stories about my dad on tour, and by the time another half hour had passed, the scary feeling of not knowing what was happening had gone, and I was in love with my father's best friend.

When we climbed down from the treehouse, when my mom cried with relief and Dad opened his arms, I looked up at Leo, wanting to stay with him, to laugh with him rather than face the reality of what I knew was happening with my parents.

He gave me a reassuring smile. "You're going to be all right, kid." And he ruffled my hair.

Yeah. To him, I'm still that twelve-year-old girl. Will he ever notice that I'm a woman?

Get your copy here
mybook.to/SSProtectingHisBestFriendsDaughter

BOOKS BY SADIE KING

Sunset Coast

Underground Crows MC

Sunset Security

Men of the Sea

The Thief's Lover

The Henchman's Obsession

The Hitman's Redemption

Maple Springs

Men of Maple Mountain

All the Single Dads

Candy's Café

Small Town Sisters

Kings County

Kings of Fire

King's Cops

For a full list of titles check out the Sadie King website

www.authorsadieking.com

GET YOUR FREE BOOK

Sign up to the Sadie King mailing list for a FREE book!

You'll be the first to hear about exclusive offers, bonus content and all the news from Sadie King.

To claim your free book visit:
www.authorsadieking.com/free

ABOUT THE AUTHOR

Sadie King is a USA Today Best Selling Author of short instalove romance.
She lives in New Zealand with her ex-military husband and raucous young son.

Follow Sadie King on BookBub to get an alert whenever she has a new release, preorder, or discount!

www.bookbub.com/authors/sadie-king

www.authorsadieking.com

Printed in Great Britain
by Amazon